First Edition
ISBN-13: 978-1475235814
ISBN-10: 147523581X

Published in the United States by Xist Publishing
www.xistpublishing.com
PO Box 61593 Irvine, CA 92602

xist Publishing

Time for Bed, Bunny!

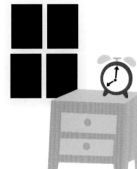

by Brenda Ponnay

Bunny, time to
get your pajamas on.

Bunny, don't forget to
put your toys away.

Bunny, where are your pajamas?

Bunny?

Not those pajamas, Bunny.

Not those either, Bunny.

That's better, Bunny.

Did you brush
your teeth, Bunny?

With toothpaste, Bunny.

Not too much, Bunny.

Bunny, get down from there!

Bunny, don't leave a mess.

Bunny, don't forget
to get a drink of water.

Go put dry pajamas on, Bunny.

Um, no.

Bunny, is that necessary?

Please pick up the mess,
Bunny.

Bunny, time to
pick out stories.

Not that many stories, Bunny.

That's more like it.

Story time is over, Bunny.
Time for bed.

IN bed, Bunny.

Lights out, Bunny.

Goodnight, Bunny.

Goodnight.

About the Author

Brenda Ponnay is the author and illustrator of several children's books including the Secret Agent Josephine series: ABC's, Colors and Numbers. She lives in Southern California with her daughter, Bug* who inspires her daily.

You can read all about their crazy adventures on her personal blog: www.secret-agent-josephine.com.

*Not her real name.

Made in the USA
Lexington, KY
25 November 2017